PUFFIN BOOKS
ANIMALS ON THE TRAIN

Born in Kasauli (Himachal Pradesh) in 1934, Ruskin Bond grew up in Jamnagar (Gujarat), Dehradun, New Delhi and Simla. His first novel, *The Room on the Roof*, which was written when he was seventeen, received the John Llewellyn Rhys Memorial Prize in 1957. Since then, he has written over 500 short stories, essays, novellas (including *The Adventures of Rusty* and *The Room of Many Colours*) and more than seventy books for children.

He received the Sahitya Akademi Award for English writing in India in 1992, the Padma Shri in 1999 and the Padma Bhushan in 2014. He lives in Landour, Mussoorie, with his extended family.

ALSO IN PUFFIN BY RUSKIN BOND

Getting Granny's Glasses
Earthquake
The Cherry Tree
The Eyes of the Eagle
Dust on the Mountain
Cricket for the Crocodile
The Tree Lover
The Day Grandfather Tickled a Tiger
White Mice
Ranji the Music Maker
Mukesh Starts a Zoo
The Wind on Haunted Hill
Puffin Classics: The Room on the Roof
Puffin Classics: Vagrants in the Valley
The Room of Many Colours: A Treasury of Stories for Children
Panther's Moon and Other Stories
The Hidden Pool
The Parrot Who Wouldn't Talk and Other Stories
Mr Oliver's Diary
Escape from Java and Other Tales of Danger
Crazy Times with Uncle Ken
The Puffin Book of Classic School Stories
The Kashmiri Storyteller
Hip-Hop Nature Boy and Other Poems
The Adventures of Rusty: Collected Stories
Thick as Thieves: Tales of Friendship
Uncles, Aunts and Elephants: A Ruskin Bond Treasury
Ranji's Wonderful Bat and Other Stories
Whispers in the Dark: A Book of Spooks
Looking for the Rainbow: My Years with Daddy
Till the Clouds Roll By: Beginning Again
Coming Round the Mountain: In the Year of Independence
A Song of India: The Year I Went Away
All-Time Favourites for Children
The Tunnel
Listen to Your Heart
All-Time Favourite Nature Stories
Animal in the House
Hold on to Your Dreams
Life's Magic Moments

Ruskin Bond

Animals on the Train

Illustrations by Saumya Oberoi

PUFFIN BOOKS
An imprint of Penguin Random House

PUFFIN BOOKS

Puffin Books is an imprint of the Penguin Random House group of companies whose addresses can be found at global.penguinrandomhouse.com

Published by Penguin Random House India Pvt. Ltd
4th Floor, Capital Tower 1, MG Road,
Gurugram 122 002, Haryana, India

This illustrated edition published in Puffin Books
by Penguin Random House 2025

Text copyright © Ruskin Bond 2025
Illustrations copyright © Saumya Oberoi 2025

All rights reserved

10 9 8 7 6 5 4 3 2 1

This is a work of fiction. Names, characters, places and incidents are either the product of the author's imagination or are used fictitiously and any resemblance to any actual person, living or dead, events or locales is entirely coincidental.

Please note that no part of this book may be used or reproduced in any manner for the purpose of training artificial intelligence technologies or systems.

ISBN 9780143428817

Typeset in Baskerville
Book design and layout by Gina James
Printed at Paras Offset Pvt. Ltd., Kundli (Haryana)

This book is sold subject to the condition that it shall not, by way of trade or otherwise, be lent, resold, hired out, or otherwise circulated without the publisher's prior consent in any form of binding or cover other than that in which it is published and without a similar condition including this condition being imposed on the subsequent purchaser.

www.penguin.co.in

A big thank you to Sohini Mitra, Simran Kaur and Prerna Chatterjee from the Puffin editorial team; to Gina James for her design work; and to Saumya Oberoi for her wonderful illustrations of the people and animals in this favourite story of mine.

Chapter 1

'ALL ABOARD!' shrieked Popeye, Grandmother's pet parrot, as the family climbed aboard the Lucknow Express. We were moving from Dehra to Lucknow, in northern India, and as Grandmother had insisted on taking her parrot along, Grandfather and I had insisted on bringing our pets—Grandfather's teenaged tiger and my small squirrel. But we thought it prudent to leave the python behind.

In those days, the trains in India were not so crowded, and it was possible to travel with a variety of creatures. Grandfather had decided to do things in style by travelling first class, so we had a four-berth compartment of our own. Timothy, the tiger, had an entire berth to himself. He was about three months old and the size of a terrier, but much stronger.

Later, everyone agreed that Timothy behaved perfectly throughout the journey. Even the guard admitted that he could not have asked for a better passenger: no stealing from vendors, no shouting at porters, no breaking of railway property and no spitting on the platform.

All the same, the journey was not without its share of incidents. Before we reached Lucknow, there was excitement enough for everyone. To begin with, Popeye objected to vendors and other people poking their hands through the windows. Before the train had moved out of the station, he had nipped two fingers and tweaked a ticket inspector's ear.

And no sooner had the train started moving than Chips, my squirrel, emerged from the pocket to examine his surroundings. Before I could stop him, he was out of the compartment door, scurrying along the corridor.

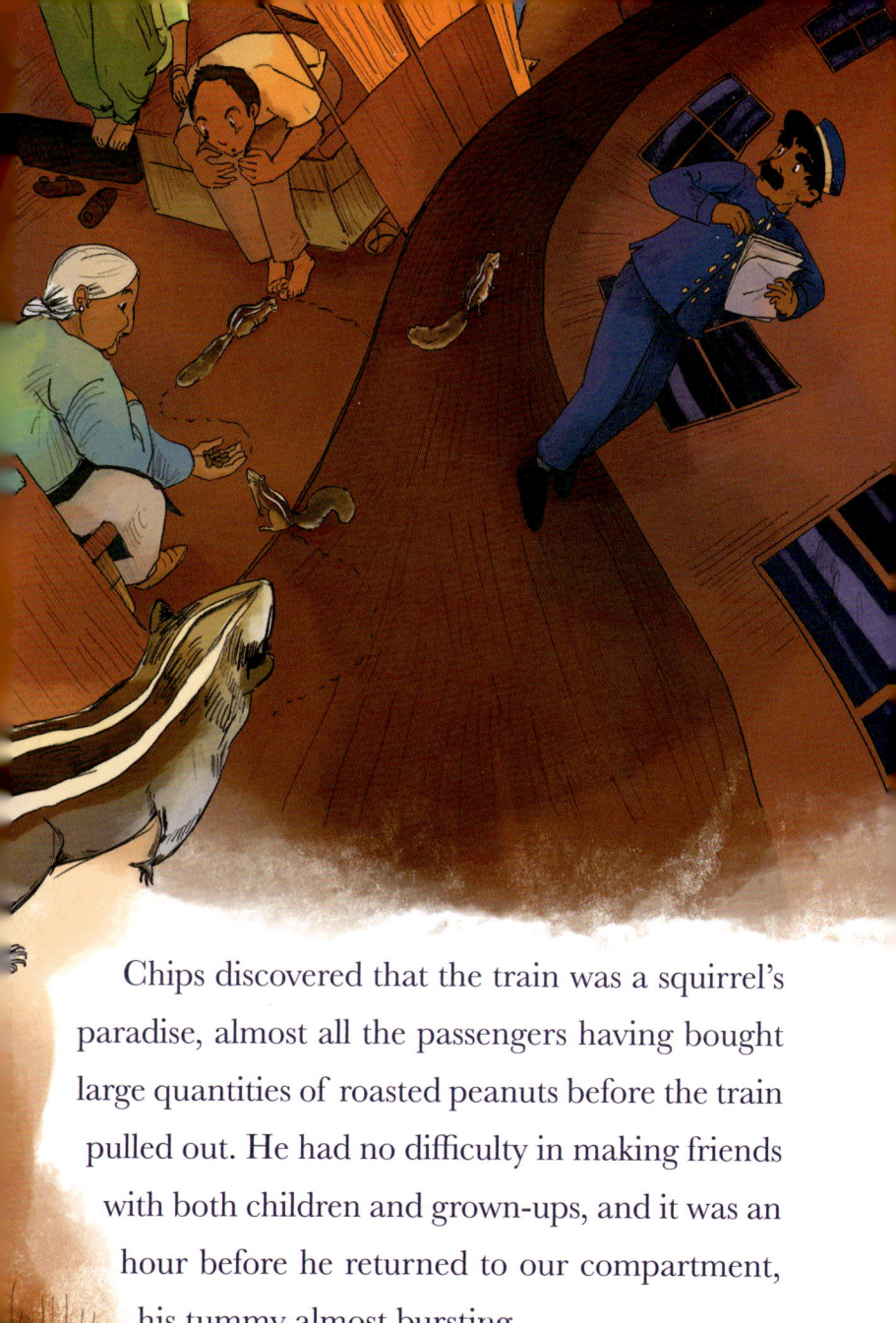

Chips discovered that the train was a squirrel's paradise, almost all the passengers having bought large quantities of roasted peanuts before the train pulled out. He had no difficulty in making friends with both children and grown-ups, and it was an hour before he returned to our compartment, his tummy almost bursting.

'I think I'll go to sleep,' said Grandmother, covering herself with a blanket and stretching out on the berth opposite Timothy's. 'It's been a tiring day.'

'Aren't you going to eat anything?' asked Grandfather.

'I'm not hungry—I had some soup before we left. You two help yourselves from the tiffin-basket.'

Chapter 2

Grandmother dozed off, and even Popeye started nodding, lulled to sleep by the clackety-clack of the wheels and the steady puffing of the steam engine.

'Well, I'm hungry,' I said. 'What did Granny make for us?'

'Sandwiches, boiled eggs and roast chicken. It's all in the tiffin-basket under your berth.'

I tugged at the large basket and dragged it into the centre of the compartment. The straps were loosely tied. No sooner had I undone them than the lid flew open, and I let out a gasp.

In the basket was Grandfather's pet python, curled up contentedly on the remains of our dinner. Grandmother had insisted that we leave the python behind, and Grandfather had let it loose in the garden. Somehow, it had managed to smuggle itself into the tiffin-basket.

'Well, what are you staring at?' asked Grandfather from his corner.

'It's the python,' I said. 'And it's finished all our dinner.'

Grandfather joined me, and together we looked down at what remained of the food. Pythons don't chew, they swallow; outlined along the length of the large snake's sleek body were the distinctive shapes of chicken and six boiled eggs. We couldn't make out the sandwiches, but presumably these had been eaten too because there was no sign of them in the basket.

Grandfather snapped the basket shut and pushed it back beneath the berth.

'We mustn't let Grandmother see him,' he said. 'She might think we brought him along on purpose.'

'Well, I'm hungry,' I complained. Just then, Chips returned from one of his forays and presented me with a peanut.

'Thanks,' I said. 'If you keep bringing me peanuts all night, I might last until morning.'

Chapter 3

It was not long before I felt sleepy. Grandfather had begun to nod off as well. The only one who was wide awake was the squirrel, still intent on investigating distant compartments.

A little after midnight, there was a great clamour at the end of the corridor. Grandfather and I woke up. Timothy growled in his sleep, and Popeye made complaining noises.

Suddenly, there were cries of 'snake, snake!'

Grandfather was on his feet in a moment. He looked under the berth. The tiffin-basket was empty.

'The python's out!' he exclaimed and dashed out of our compartment in his pyjamas. I was close behind.

About a dozen passengers were bunched together outside the washroom door.

'Anything wrong?' asked Grandfather casually.

'We can't get into the toilet,' someone complained. 'There's a huge snake inside.'

'Let me take a look,' said Grandfather. 'I know all about snakes.'

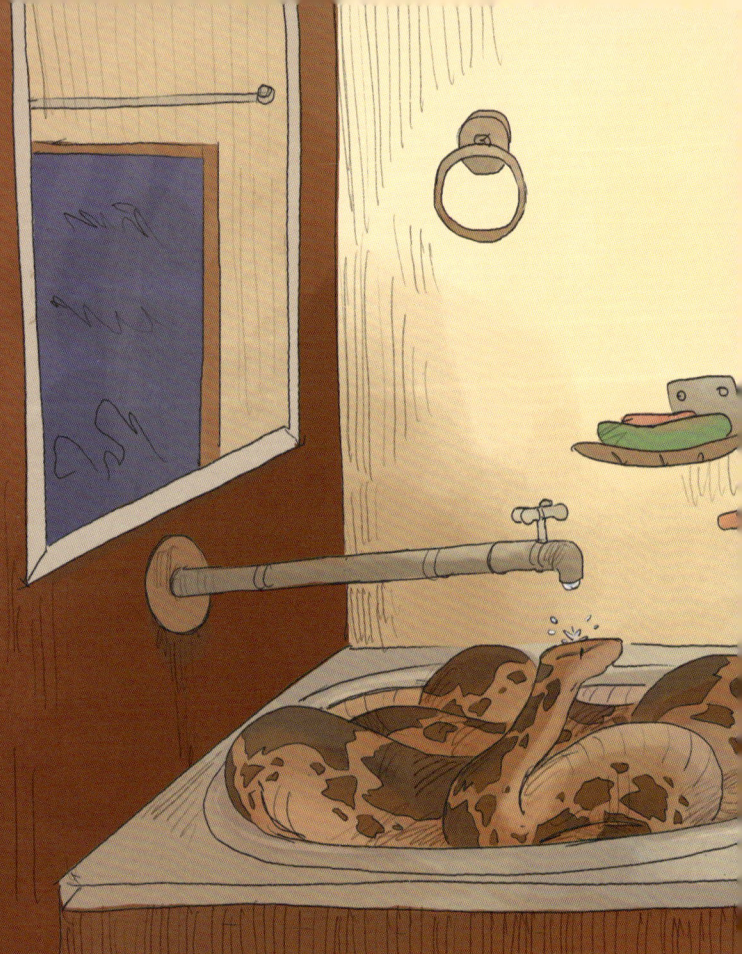

The passengers made way for him, and he entered the washroom to find the python curled up in the washbasin. After its heavy meal, the snake had become thirsty and, finding the lid of the tiffin-basket easy to pry up, had set out in search of water.

Grandfather gathered up the sleepy, overfed python and stepped out of the washroom. The passengers hastily made way for them.

'Nothing to worry about,' said grandfather cheerfully. 'It's just a harmless young python. He's had his dinner already, so no one is in any danger!' And he marched back to our compartment with the python in his arms. As soon as I was inside, he bolted the door.

Grandmother was sitting up on her berth. 'I knew you'd do something foolish behind my back,' she scolded. 'You told me you'd got rid of that creature, and all this time you've been hiding it from me.'

Grandfather tried to explain that he had nothing to do with it, that the python had smuggled itself into the tiffin-basket, but Grandmother was unconvinced. She declared that Grandfather couldn't live without the creature and that he had deliberately brought it along.

'What will Mabel do when she sees it!' cried Grandmother despairingly.

My Aunt Mabel was a schoolteacher in Lucknow. She was going to share our new house, and she was terrified of all reptiles, particularly snakes.

'We won't let her see it,' said Grandfather. 'Back it goes into the tiffin-basket.'

Chapter 4

Early next morning, the train steamed into Lucknow. Aunt Mabel was on the platform to receive us.

Grandfather let all the other passengers get off before he emerged from the compartment with Timothy on a leash. I had Chips in my pocket, a suitcase in both hands. Popeye stayed perched on Grandmother's shoulder, eyeing the busy platform with considerable mistrust.

Aunt Mabel, a lover of good food, immediately spotted the tiffin-basket, picked it up and said, 'It's not very heavy. I'll carry it out to the taxi. I hope you've kept something for me.'

'A whole chicken,' I said.

'We hardly ate anything,' said Grandfather.

'It's all yours, Aunty!' I added.

'Oh, good!' exclaimed Aunt Mabel. 'It's been ages since I tasted something cooked by your grandmother.' And after that, there was no getting the basket away from her.

Glancing at it, I thought I saw the lid bulge, but Grandfather had tied it down quite firmly this time, and there was little likelihood of it suddenly bursting open.

An enormous old taxi was waiting outside the station, and the family tumbled into it. Timothy got into the back seat, leaving enough room for Grandfather and me. Aunt Mabel sat up in front with Grandmother, the tiffin-basket on her lap.

'I'm dying to see what's inside,' she said. 'Can't I take just a little peek?'

'Not now,' said Grandfather. 'First, let's enjoy the breakfast you've got waiting for us.'

'Yes, wait until we get home,' said Grandmother. 'Now tell the taxi driver where to take us, dear. He's looking rather nervous.'

Aunt Mabel gave the driver instructions, and the taxi shot off in a cloud of dust.

'Well, here we go!' said Grandfather. 'I'm looking forward to settling into the new house.'

Popeye, perched proudly on Grandmother's shoulder and kept a suspicious eye on the quivering tiffin-basket.

'All aboard!' he squawked. 'All aboard!'

When we got to our new house, we found a light breakfast waiting for us on the dining table.

'It isn't much,' said Aunt Mabel. 'But we'll supplement it with the contents of your hamper.' And placing the basket on the table, she removed the lid.

The python was half-asleep, its head resting against the basket. Aunt Mabel fainted away.

Grandfather promptly picked up the python, took it into the garden and draped it over the branch of a guava tree.

When Aunt Mabel recovered, she insisted that there was a huge snake in the tiffin-basket. We showed her the empty basket.

'You're seeing things,' said Grandfather.

'It must be the heat,' I said.

Grandmother said nothing.

But Popeye broke into shrieks of maniacal laughter, and soon, everyone, including a slightly hysterical Aunt Mabel, was doubled over with laughter.

Scan QR code to access the
Penguin Random House India website